CLIFFORD'S REALLY BIG MOVIE™

THE STAR OF THE SHOW

Adapted by Dena Neusner

Illustrated by Barry Goldberg

Based on the Scholastic book series
"Clifford The Big Red Dog"
by Norman Bridwell

ISBN 0-439-62749-4

10 9 8 7 6 5 4   04 05 06 07 08

Printed in the U.S.A.
First printing, January 2004

SCHOLASTIC INC.

New York   Toronto   London   Auckland   Sydney
Mexico City   New Delhi   Hong Kong   Buenos Aires

A carnival came to Birdwell Island!

Emily Elizabeth went with Clifford.

She rode the Ferris wheel.

Clifford met T-Bone and Cleo.

"This place is the best," said T-Bone.

"There's so much food!"

"Look!" said Clifford. "An animal show!"

"Let's check it out," said Cleo.

The lights went out.

A spotlight came on.

"Hello, my name is Larry.

I am proud to present

the most amazing animals ever!"

Rodrigo lifted a barbell.

It was bigger than he was!

Dirk zoomed by on his rocket skates.

"Welcome Dorothy the High-Wire Heifer!" said

Larry. "And now here's the star of our show . . .

Shackelford the Flying Ferret!"

Shackelford swooped down on a trapeze swing.

He landed on Dorothy's head and juggled.

A balloon made Dorothy lose her balance!

"That was really good!" said T-Bone.

"Want to join our show?" asked Shackelford.

"We are entering a talent contest. The prize is all the Tummy Yummies you can eat!"

"No, thank you," said Clifford.

He did not want to leave Emily Elizabeth.

"Clifford!" called Emily Elizabeth.

"Breakfast!"

"Feeding Clifford must be a BIG

problem," said Mr. Bleakman.

"Clifford is not a problem," said

Mr. Howard. "He's family."

But Clifford didn't hear him.

"What's wrong?" asked T-Bone.

"I eat too much," said Clifford.

"I'm joining the animal show," Clifford said.

"I want to win Tummy Yummies!"

"You're not going without us!" said Cleo.

"Clifford!" called Emily Elizabeth.

"Where are you?"

"Look, paw prints!" said Charley.

"I think he left the island."

Clifford, Cleo, and T-Bone found
the carnival.
Larry was happy to see them.

"Need a home?" asked Larry.

They wagged their tails.

The next show
didn't go well.

"It's Big Red to the rescue!" said Larry.

The crowd cheered.

Dorothy told Clifford a secret.

"I'm afraid of heights," she said.

Clifford had an idea.

"Hop on!" he said.

"This isn't scary!" said Dorothy. "It's fun!"

"Welcome back to the Tummy Yummies

contest!" said the announcer.

"Clifford is on TV!" said Emily Elizabeth.

Larry's Amazing Animals
were a big success!

"And the winner is . . .

Larry's Amazing Animal Show!"

Emily Elizabeth and her parents brought
Clifford, T-Bone, and Cleo home.
Now they had enough Tummy Yummies to
last a lifetime!

Clifford stepped in a puddle.

Splash!

"Clifford!" shouted Mr. Bleakman.

But then he smiled.

"It's good to have you back, boy," he said.

"Welcome home, Clifford,"

said Emily Elizabeth.

"Woof!" said Clifford.

He was very happy to be back on Birdwell Island with all the family and friends he loved.

Do You Remember?

Circle the right answer.

1. Where did Clifford first see the animal show?
    a. At the zoo
    b. At a carnival
    c. At school

2. What scared Dorothy?
    a. Dogs
    b. Tummy Yummies
    c. Heights

Which happened first?
Which happened next?
Which happened last?

Write a 1, 2, or 3 in the space after each sentence.

Clifford swam across the ocean with Cleo and T-Bone. _____

Emily Elizabeth saw Clifford on TV. _____

Shackelford asked Clifford to join the animal show. _____

Answers: